The Haunting of Hawthorne
by Anne Schraff

Perfection Learning® Corporation
Logan, Iowa 51546

For information, contact:
Perfection Learning® Corporation
1000 North Second Avenue, P.O. Box 500,
Logan, Iowa 51546-0500.
Phone: 1-800-831-4190 • Fax: 1-800-543-2745
perfectionlearning.com

Paperback
ISBN-10: 0-7891-7539-8
ISBN-13: 978-0-7891-7539-7

Reinforced Library Binding
ISBN-10: 0-7569-8379-7
ISBN-13: 978-0-7569-8379-6

29999

6 7 8 9 10 11 PP 18 17 16 15 14 13

1 WE WERE DISCUSSING the witch trials that took place in Salem, Massachusetts. Mr. Kramer, our U.S. history teacher, told us about one old woman who was accused of being a witch. She said she was innocent and that the man who accused her was lying. She threatened that if she was hanged, the man who lied would also die.

They went ahead and hanged her anyway. And soon afterwards, the man who accused her choked to death!

"I can't believe that," Jan Draper said. Jan didn't believe much of anything.

A deep voice came from the back of the room. "I think it might be true."

I'd never heard that voice before. I turned and glanced in the newcomer's direction. Then I just sat and stared, my heart pounding like crazy.

I don't like people who stare, but I couldn't help it. He was the handsomest boy I'd ever seen. He looked like a magnificent statue.

"Well," Mr. Kramer said, "there's a lot of evidence to indicate that the man did choke to death."

"But the old woman couldn't *make* it happen," Jan said with a laugh.

"I wouldn't be so sure," the boy said in his deep voice.

My friend Dina had noticed the new boy, too. After class as we walked to our lockers, she told me what she knew about him.

"His name is Basil Harris," she said. "I heard he's a transfer student. I also heard he was the best-looking guy on the face of the planet. At least that part is right."

"I wonder where he's from?" I said.

"Someone told me that he lives with his grandmother. I guess his parents are dead."

Dina added, "I heard he's smart, too. Who knows, he could end up valedictorian? Of course, he'd have to beat you out. And *nobody* is smarter than you!"

I laughed. "Oh, Dina!"

It was true that I worked really hard and

got good grades. But the speech teacher, Ms. Brundage, made the final selection for class speakers. Just having the best grades wasn't enough. She had to like you.

I'm not one of Ms. Brundage's favorite students. I think the fact that I have epilepsy makes her nervous. That's silly because as long as I take my medication, I'm fine.

Unfortunately, Ms. Brundage keeps worrying that I'm going to have a fit or something. In my freshman year at Hawthorne High, she even suggested that I should not compete in the speech contest. She kept hinting around that I might embarrass myself "under the stress of the situation."

I guess a lot of people feel uncomfortable around things they don't understand. I know Ms. Brundage sure does.

"Look, there he goes!" Dina hissed. Then she nudged me so hard, she almost made me lose my balance.

I sneaked a quick peek and saw Basil walking toward the library.

"Hey, I bet he's really lonely being at

a new school," I said. "One of us should show him around, give him the inside facts."

"Not me," Dina protested. "I'd be too nervous." She laughed.

"Okay. I'm elected," I said, grinning happily. I guess I'm what you'd call the friendly type. My folks always say that if aliens from outer space ever landed here, I'd be the first to make friends with them.

I hurried down the hall and caught up with Basil. "Hi," I said. "I'm Valerie Moran. I'm in your history class. Maybe you didn't see me."

He smiled. "I saw you. My name's Basil Harris."

"Well—welcome to Hawthorne. Such as it is."

I glanced down the hallway. Hawthorne was once a nice school. The students used to have a lot of spirit. The buildings had been in good condition. The grass had been green, and pretty shrubs sprouted up everywhere.

· Now the kids didn't much care. The buildings were covered with graffiti, and vandals had torn up the shrubs.

"Our school is sort of run-down," I apologized. "But some of us are trying to do something about it."

"Good for you," he said.

"I'd like to show you around the school if you have time. That is, if you haven't already had the grand tour."

"Just a modest one. I could use another. I'm still a bit lost." He really seemed glad I was taking an interest in him.

I led Basil to the science building and the tiny patch of grass where I sat during lunch break. My favorite eucalyptus tree stood there, and I pointed it out to him.

"I sit under it and dream," I explained. "I think of all the places I'm going to go, all the things I'm going to do. I call it my dreaming tree."

"Everyone should have a dreaming tree," he said with a smile.

I continued with the tour, showing Basil around the rest of the school. Then I turned to him and said, "I've saved the best for last."

"What's that?"

"Come on. It's outside in front of the library." I grabbed his hand and led him to the bronze statue of William Evans Hawthorne.

We both stopped and examined the piece. It was old and dirty—it desperately needed to be cleaned. You couldn't see the face very well anymore. But for all that, it still looked very noble.

"That's William Evans Hawthorne," I explained. "He was the first principal of this school, back in the nineteenth century."

Basil slowly nodded his head. "He must have been something to have a school named after him."

"Yeah, he was. See, in 1891, there was a terrible fire in the school. Mr. Hawthorne, he saw to it that every last student got out alive. He went into that burning building time after time to get all of them out. But then he was killed himself. A beam fell on him."

I stared up at the statue again. "The fire completely destroyed the old building. When they rebuilt it, they gave

Mr. Hawthorne the nicest tribute they could think of. They named it after him."

"He must have cared about his students very much," Basil said quietly.

"Yeah. It's a shame his school looks so crummy now. It never used to be like this. All the litter and graffiti."

The sound of the bell interrupted us. Since both Basil and I had classes next period, we said goodbye to each other.

I didn't see Basil again the rest of the day. Then, after school, I saw him heading out towards the parking lot. I was about to call to him when a car came skidding around the corner.

I guessed who the driver was at once. It had to be Bob Short. He loved to drag race around the school. He was a born show-off.

I suddenly realized that Bob's car was out of control. I could see he was fighting the wheel. Horrified, I watched as the car headed right for a bunch of kids waiting for the school bus!

At the last minute, Bob swerved sharply and missed the kids.

I breathed a huge sigh of relief and ran up to where Basil was standing. We watched as Bob pulled up to the curb and stuck his head out the window.

"Had you going there for a minute, huh?" he said with a laugh.

He was met with a chorus of yells and curses. "Damn you, Short," one boy yelled. "I'm calling the cops!"

I met Basil's eyes. He shook his head. "A fool like that shouldn't be allowed to hold a license."

Bob heard the remark. He glared at Basil. "Mind your own business, idiot!"

To my amazement, Basil didn't get mad. He just said, "You better stay away from cars for a while. You'll die in that car if you don't watch out."

At that moment, a police car drove up. Apparently someone else had already reported Bob Short's antics. Bob was ticketed, which only made him angrier. I saw him race away from school after the police left, burning rubber as he pulled away.

I said goodbye to Basil and climbed on

my bike and headed home. On the way I stopped and bought myself a cola. Just as I began pedaling home again, I heard a siren over on Highland Avenue. An uneasy feeling crept over me. Suddenly I wished there were a quicker way home than down that street.

When I reached the corner of Highland and 32nd, I found a crowd of people gathered there. I could see from their faces that something terrible had happened. I pulled up and stopped.

I spotted the ambulance almost at once. My eyes were drawn to its throbbing red light. A sick feeling began to grow in the pit of my stomach.

Then I saw the car: a brand new, bright red convertible. I'd only seen one like it in town, and that belonged to Bob Short. Bob's father had given it to him on his sixteenth birthday. I guess Bob's parents sort of spoiled him.

Now the little car was smashed up against a semi.

"I saw the whole thing," a lady told me. "The light changed to red. The truck stopped, but the sports car didn't. I guess he couldn't, he was going so fast. And then—oh, it was horrible. He ran right into the back of the truck!"

I sat down on the curb. My legs were shaking so much that they wouldn't hold me. The woman didn't say, but I knew anyway. Bob Short was dead.

I'd never liked Bob. He was like a lot of kids at Hawthorne. He wrote on the walls. He didn't care about the school. He didn't care about other people. Once I even saw him smash one of the school windows.

But I had known Bob ever since junior high. He was part of my life. And now he was lying on a stretcher with a sheet over his face.

I watched numbly as two men picked up the stretcher and loaded it into the ambulance. They walked slowly. There was no hurry now.

I remembered what Basil had said earlier. *You better stay away from cars for a while. You'll die in that car if you don't watch out.* The words seemed so eerie now.

I picked up my bike and headed home. As I quickly cycled away from the dreadful scene, tears began to fill my eyes. It seemed strange to cry for Bob Short. It didn't make sense. But I couldn't help it.

I cried all the way home.

2 WHEN I GOT home, Dad's car was in the driveway. That upset me even more. Maybe they'd laid him off. Lately he'd been worrying a lot about losing his job.

I hurried into the house. "Hi, Dad," I said, studying his face to see if something were wrong. He looked tired. "You're home early today."

To my relief, he smiled and explained, "We finished ahead of schedule." Then he took a closer look at my face. "Honey, what is it? You've been crying."

"Oh, Dad, I saw something really awful when I was coming home. Bob Short was killed in a car accident."

Dad's eyes widened in shock. "Bob Short? Isn't he the boy who was stopped for driving without a license a couple months ago?"

"Yeah. It was just a horrible accident. You know what's so strange, though? There's a new boy at school. His name is

Basil Harris. Just about an hour before Bob was killed, he sort of said it would happen."

"Well, I guess anybody who saw the way Bob drove could have predicted trouble ahead," Dad said. He shook his head sadly. "I feel sorry for Bob's folks. He was an only child, you know."

I sat down on our lumpy old sofa. Up till now, I'd just been thinking about Bob. Now I began to consider how his family would take this.

"I wish I could do something for his parents. Maybe I'll buy a card for the Shorts and ask all the kids to sign it."

"That would be really thoughtful," Dad said.

I nodded. I wished I could remember something nice about Bob. I couldn't though. For a long time he'd been part of a group of troublemakers led by Dennie Plover. A lot of popular kids belonged to the group. Even our student council president, Jim Argus, was a member.

Everyone in this group competed to see how much trouble they could make without getting kicked out of school. They ruined classes, cheated on tests, mocked other kids, and trashed the school.

Despite my memories of Bob, I still wanted to go ahead with my plan. So the next day I brought a card to school and got the kids to sign it. Some even chipped in money for flowers.

During the announcements, they said that the student officers were going to the funeral with the principal. Jim Argus laughed when he heard. "That means I get to miss chemistry and English class," he said.

"Man, some friend you are!" Dina exclaimed. "Bob is dead, and you're laughing it up like his funeral is just another holiday."

Jim sneered. "He was a jerk."

"Give the dead a little respect," Basil said. I hadn't seen him approach.

Jim shot Basil a dirty look. "Look, you just got here, remember? I don't need a lecture from a transfer student. Maybe you don't know it, but I'm student council president here."

"If I were you, I wouldn't brag about being president," Basil said sharply.

"This school looks like it's been hit by a bomb. And you could mistake this campus for a garbage dump. Now you're laughing about a dead person. Well, I can't see why you were ever elected to anything."

Jim's face twisted with anger. He began cursing Basil with every word he could think of. Basil just smiled and walked away.

I stared after him in amazement. Then I turned to Dina. She was smiling broadly. "Well, Jim, he sure found out fast what's going on around here!" she crowed.

"If you don't like me as president," Jim snarled, "why don't you get somebody else?" Then he stalked off.

"Hey, that's an idea!" Dina said. Her eyes began to gleam.

"What do you mean?"

"Let's have a recall election, Val! Listen, I know it's legal, too, because I did a report for journalism class on the council rules."

"You mean it?" I said excitedly.

"Sure. If we don't do something fast, we'll be remembered as the worst senior class in Hawthorne's history. Do we want to graduate from Apathy and Litter High?"

She snapped her fingers. "Hey, I got an idea! Let's run Basil after we dump Argus. Basil is just different and exciting enough to get everybody's attention!"

"But nobody knows Basil," I objected.

Before Dina could answer, the bell rang. I had music class, so I told Dina I'd talk to her later. Then I hurried off, anxious not to be late. Mrs. Gottsman was furious when anyone was late. She was a great music teacher, but she was tough.

I was happily surprised to find Basil in my class. He waved a hand and I went to sit beside him.

"Maybe you'll bring me good luck," he said. "I'll be singing for Mrs. Gottsman for the first time today. I hope I'm good enough for the choir."

"Well, if you sing anything like you speak, you'll be fine," I assured him.

A few minutes after class started, Mrs. Gottsman asked Basil to do a solo.

He calmly stood up and began his song. For the next few minutes, the only sounds in the room were the piano and Basil's rich, full voice. I sat frozen, listening to one of the most beautiful performances I'd ever heard.

"What a magnificent solo!" Mrs. Gottsman said when he finished.

Everybody in the class applauded. Everybody except Dennie and Jan that is. I figured Jim Argus had already told them what Basil had said. That bunch really stuck together. Until you were dead, that is—like poor Bob Short.

As we left class, I said to Basil, "You sing like a professional!"

"I enjoy singing. And I think I'll like Mrs. Gottsman for a teacher."

"She can be crabby," I said, "but she's a real artist."

I knew that some of the kids made fun of Mrs. Gottsman behind her back. She was the oldest teacher at Hawthorne and her clothes were old-fashioned.

I told Basil as much as I knew about Mrs. Gottsman. "She was born in

Germany. During the war, she was in a Nazi concentration camp. One of the guards injured her hands. If it hadn't been for that, she might have been a famous pianist."

Basil nodded. "You can see in her eyes how much she's suffered. It's like she's been through fire, but her spirit has managed to survive."

I stared at Basil, a little awed. I'd never known a guy like him before. He was much older in his ways than any of the other guys I knew.

"You are really different, Basil," I finally blurted out.

He grinned. "I hope that's good."

"Oh, yeah, it is." I stared into his deep black eyes for a moment. A sudden memory struck me, and I smiled. "By the way, I should warn you that Dina is plotting something. She wants to recall Jim Argus and have a new election. She thinks you should run for student council president."

"Yeah? Well, if the students want to elect me, I'd sure try to turn this school around," Basil said. I was really surprised. I thought he'd turn the idea down cold.

"You mean you'd run?" I asked.

"Sure. Argus isn't good for this school. And I think Hawthorne could be a much better place. There are a lot of good kids here from what I've seen. Why shouldn't we try to make this school into something?" There was real excitement in his voice.

"Basil, that's great! Why, that sounds like the opening lines of a campaign speech!"

He laughed and we promised to talk later about the election. Then I headed out for Mr. Prager's English class. Mr. Prager was also my homeroom teacher.

When I came in the classroom, he said, "Valerie, I have the scholarship papers you wanted."

"Thanks, Mr. Prager." I took the application and went to my desk to study it.

This scholarship was for students who wanted to be teachers. Ever since I'd been in fourth grade, that had been my dream—to teach, especially disabled kids. I wanted to help the disabled to do as much in life as they could.

I guess that having epilepsy made me even more determined. I know how being different can hurt. The hardest thing is proving to people that you can do as well as anybody else.

I scanned the pages of the application. It looked pretty involved. Besides filling out information on family background, I had to write an essay saying why I wanted to teach. Later I'd have to take a current affairs test. The committee would also want a record of my grades and college entrance exams scores.

I felt a little overwhelmed by all the work. But I really needed this scholarship. My folks couldn't begin to pay the bills for college.

After English, I met Dina in the hall. She eagerly pushed some papers at me. I couldn't believe it! She already had a bunch of signatures for the recall election.

"I'm going to tell Jim Argus how many I've got," Dina declared. "Maybe he'll be smart enough to resign. Even he should know when he's beat!"

I hurried off to history class to tell Basil the news. Then he noticed my scholarship application and asked about it. I explained and told him about all the hurdles to qualifying. "I have to get the top score on the current affairs exam. It's always a real tough test."

"You'll get the best grade," Basil said.

I shot a curious gaze at Basil. He didn't know that much about me. Yet he'd made his prediction as if he were sure.

"Basil, how come you sound so positive?" I asked.

"Because I *am* positive," he said firmly.

I shook my head and tried to laugh it off. "So do you have ESP or something?"

He hesitated long enough to make me wonder. "Something like that," he finally said.

I wasn't sure how to take any of this. Maybe it was just Basil's rich voice and his fascinating eyes. But I was halfway convinced he was telling me the truth.

"Come on, Basil. Really?"

"Yeah, really." He didn't seem to want to say anything more about it. But I guess he saw how puzzled I was, so he added, "It's not that amazing. There are a lot of examples of people knowing things before they happen. It's called precognition."

"Yes, I know about that," I said. But I'd never known anyone before who could really predict the future. And I wasn't sure if I believed in precognition or not.

The door opened then, and a substitute teacher came in. She was a slim, young woman and she looked nervous.

"My name is Ms. Walters," she said. "I'll be your history teacher while Mr. Kramer is at a workshop."

Immediately the troublemakers were on their toes. Dennie's face lit up as soon as he heard Ms. Walters' southern drawl.

"Yas, ma'am," he said, mocking her accent.

"I understand you are reading *Gone with the Wind*," Ms. Walters said.

"We sure is," Dennie murmured. Ms. Walters didn't hear him. But most of the kids did and many laughed.

"Knock it off," Basil whispered.

Dennie gave Basil a dirty look in return.

"You know, you can choke changing your voice like that," Basil warned.

Dennie just laughed.

"Has this class seen the movie *Gone with the Wind*?" Ms. Walters asked.

"We sure did see it, yas, ma'am," Dennie mocked.

The kids around him were now laughing wildly.

And then Dennie began to cough. Soon he was gasping for breath, grabbing at his throat. His eyes began to bulge wildly. They looked like they were going to pop out of his head.

Abruptly he got up and ran from the classroom. I guess he went to get a drink of water.

Ms. Walters went out of the room to check on him. When she came back in, she looked a little upset and lost. "Well, where were we?" she asked.

"You were asking about the movie. I think the book was much better," Basil said. "I feel the character of Scarlett was distorted in the movie."

The class discussion was good after that. But I couldn't really pay attention to it. Basil had warned Dennie that he would choke if he mocked Ms. Walters. And he had! *Just like Bob Short had his car accident.*

After class I caught up with Basil in the library. He was taking down some notes from a book.

I looked at his handwriting. It was delicate and old-fashioned looking. I'd never seen anybody write like that, except my great-grandmother.

"You sure write nicely," I said.

"Thank you." He smiled as he said it. Yet there always seemed something so serious about his face. His intense eyes strengthened that impression.

I remembered some old family photos I'd looked over for a research paper. It suddenly struck me that Basil looked like those people from another century.

Perhaps Basil only seemed different because he lived with his grandmother.

Maybe he'd been raised under the rules of another generation. Yet how to explain his weird ability to predict things?

"Basil, that was odd—the way Dennie began to choke—" I hesitantly suggested.

"Yes, wasn't it?" Basil said calmly.

I smiled nervously. "I guess that's what they call the power of suggestion, huh? I mean, you said he would choke if he mocked Ms. Walters—and he did."

"I guess that's right," Basil said.

On the face of it, his answer was pretty ordinary. But I had a strange feeling that Basil knew more than he was telling—a strange feeling that he wasn't like the rest of us at Hawthorne High. He seemed different in a way that scared me a little.

3 BY THE NEXT morning, Dina had more news for me about the recall election. I caught up with her before school. She was standing talking to Basil in the hall.

When she saw me, Dina shouted, "We did it! Jim is going to resign. Can you believe it? He saw all the signatures, and he knew there was no point fighting. And the principal agreed to let us nominate new candidates in homeroom tomorrow. So guess who I'm nominating?"

We both grinned at Basil, and he bowed. "I'm honored," he said.

Just then Jan came walking by. She was wearing an expensive sweater and matching skirt. She looked really pretty and she knew it.

Jan gave Basil a melting smile. I immediately knew what was up. Undoubtedly she wanted to add Basil to her list of conquests.

Jan wasn't one of your one-man women.

She wanted every guy in school to be crazy about her.

"I heard about Jim resigning, Basil," she said in her phony, sexy voice. "I also heard you were running. Well, you've got my support, Basil."

I almost laughed. What a hypocrite she was! She didn't care what happened to the school. She just wanted to snare Basil.

"Well, I need all the support I can get," Basil said. He sort of smiled. I couldn't tell if he was impressed with Jan or not. But I guess just about any guy would be impressed with a girl who was that pretty.

Basil took off shortly after that. As soon as he was out of earshot, Jan exclaimed, "He's gorgeous! I wonder if he's going with anybody to the homecoming dance?"

"I thought you were going with Jim Argus," I said.

Jan laughed. "I can go with anybody I like. Jim doesn't own me. Nobody does."

What Jan said was true, and that depressed me. Jan flirted with any and every guy she liked. Yet she rarely wore anybody's ring for long.

I swallowed my disappointment. I had sort of hoped that Basil might take me to the dance. But deep down, I figured he would be as attracted to Jan as every other guy. If he had a chance to go with Jan, he'd grab it.

I tried not to think about my silly dream romance with Basil. I decided to stay tuned to all the lectures and shut out thoughts of Basil.

In music class, Dennie Plover helped distract me. Dennie was back in class after his choking episode and seemed okay. At least okay enough to pull his usual stupid tricks.

Dennie had a good voice, but he didn't sing much. He was too lazy to learn anything well. Today he wasn't bothering to sing at all.

About ten minutes into class, Mrs. Gottman stopped us. "You're not singing with the rest of us," she said to Dennie.

"Vot?" Dennie asked in a loud voice. He was imitating Mrs. Gottsman's accent.

Mrs. Gottsman flushed. "I want to know why you are not singing!"

"I was singing," he protested. "Maybe you just couldn't hear me. You a little deaf, huh?"

I saw Basil whisper something to Dennie. Dennie just laughed.

"Either sing with the rest of the class or come in after school," Mrs. Gottsman warned. "All right, now let's practice our program for the holiday assembly," Mrs. Gottsman said. "Which song shall we do first?"

"How about 'Ober der River'?" Dennie said in an obnoxious way.

And then a strange thing happened. Dennie began pulling at his collar as if it were too tight. He seemed to be choking on something. He finally got up and left the room.

"Mrs. Gottsman, you'll have to excuse Dennie. I think he's sick," Basil said.

I stared in disbelief at Basil. The whole incident was just like yesterday.

After class, I went to the nurse's office.

I had to find out what was wrong with Dennie.

I saw him still sitting there on the cot,

looking weak and puzzled. As I started for the door, the school nurse came charging out. She looked angry. I heard her mumble as she passed, "I've never heard anything so ridiculous in my life!"

I peeked around the door of the office. "Hey, Dennie," I called. "What's the matter with you?"

"I can hardly breathe, that's what's the matter with me!" Dennie croaked.

"Is it an allergic reaction? Did you eat something different for lunch?"

"Allergy? It's Harris—he did it!" Dennie muttered.

"Basil?" My heart skipped a couple of beats. "What are you talking about?" I asked, though of course I suspected what he meant.

"He made me choke!" Dennie said. "I swear it! He threatened me. Then I started choking! It was like somebody had me by the throat."

"Dennie, that's crazy. It's impossible," I said. But I wasn't so sure.

Dennie clutched at his throat. "My throat is still numb. He did it. That Harris guy used some kind of—magic on me!"

"You better not tell people stuff like that," I said. "They'll think you're crazy. It's just the power of suggestion, that's all. Basil warned you that you'd choke if you didn't stop mocking Mrs. Gottsman. He sort of hypnotized you."

Dennie didn't reply. But I could see he halfway believed me.

I talked to Dennie a little bit longer, trying to reassure him. Then I left after Mr. Plover came to take him home.

Later that day, after history class, I went to study hall. As I had hoped, I found Basil there reading. When I sat down at his table, he glanced up and smiled.

"Well, how did you do that?" I asked.

"Oh, you mean about Dennie?" he calmly asked. Instead of answering, he said, "I didn't like watching him upset Mrs. Gottsman."

"I never knew anyone before who could make people believe stuff like that."

"It's nothing much. Just the power of suggestion. But it was great to see how Mrs. Gottsman's eyes lit up after he left.

She has so much to give the class. It would be a shame to miss it because of somebody like Plover. He's such a scoundrel."

I laughed. "A scoundrel?"

"Sure. You know what a scoundrel is, don't you?"

"Yeah. I just never heard anybody use the word in conversation before. I've read it in old books. It means 'a rotten person.'" I hesitated for a minute. Then I asked, "Basil, promise you won't laugh if I tell you something?"

"Promise," he replied.

"Well, you sort of remind me of people from another time. I mean, I can just see you riding in a carriage pulled by four shiny black horses. Or waltzing around a huge ballroom." I knew it sounded crazy, but it was true. "Even your handwriting is old-fashioned."

"I take that as a compliment, Valerie. I like the past—especially the nineteenth century. It seems to me that people were more gracious then. The little kindnesses were more important to them. It was just a nicer time."

I thought quietly for a moment about what Basil said. It was strange how his words always seemed to move me or convince me. There was an eerie power in his voice.

The image of Dennie still struggling for breath returned to my mind. Had he felt Basil's power, too?

I couldn't let the thought go. "Basil—about Dennie. Did you sort of hypnotize him into thinking he was choking?" I asked.

"Sort of." He grinned then. "Maybe I'm a wizard."

"Oh, Basil!"

"Sure, I'll put a spell on the whole school so they'll elect me president."

"Come on!" I laughed.

When the period was over, I went to speech class. Class ran smoothly for me until Ms. Brundage asked to see me afterwards.

When the bell rang, I reluctantly went up to her desk. I knew I couldn't be in any trouble with my grades. But talking to Ms. Brundage always made me uneasy.

"Valerie," she said, "I just learned you're one of the students competing for the teaching scholarship."

"Yes, I am," I said.

Ms. Brundage nodded. "Look, Valerie, you're a bright girl and a hard worker. But I think you should know that the current affairs test is very tough and long. It's a three-hour exam. It can be quite a strain."

I felt the anger rising in me. Did Ms. Brundage think tough test problems brought on epileptic attacks?

Then I remembered that if I won the scholarship, it would be presented at an assembly. A lot of important people would be there. Ms. Brundage was probably afraid I'd have an epileptic fit and disgrace the school.

I wanted to lash out at Ms. Brundage's narrow-mindedness. But all I said was, "I don't mind taking the test."

"Valerie, I'm honestly thinking of you. I just want to prepare you for the possibility of failure and—well, embarrassment, that's all."

"Thank you, Ms. Brundage, but I'll

be fine," I said coldly. Embarrassment? Embarrassment for me or for her?

I swallowed my fury. Rather than argue, I just left the room.

I got another blow to my pride when I left school that day. As I passed the parking lot, I saw Jan talking to Basil by his motorcycle. She was smiling and speaking softly. Well, I thought, there goes Basil Harris. Another trophy on Jan's wall!

* * *

The election heated up really fast. The next day Basil's name was entered for student council president. Another guy and a girl were nominated, too.

After about a week of campaigning, we had a special assembly, and the three candidates all made speeches. The guy just promised to do his best, and the girl said she'd try to improve school spirit. They were pretty run-of-the-mill speeches.

But then Basil got up. My heart started beating faster.

"When I first came to this school," Basil began, "a friend showed me the statue of the man this school is named for. Most schools are named for presidents or great writers or poets. But this school is named for a man who loved his students so much that he gave his life for them. I can't think of a greater sacrifice—or a greater name for this school."

There was a lot of applause. Then Basil continued, "I took a walk around school yesterday, and I was disappointed by what I saw.

"I looked at the walls and desks and sidewalks, and I saw obscenities scrawled everywhere.

"I looked around the campus, and I saw litter where flowers should be.

"I looked around the classrooms, and I saw good teachers tired of trying to talk to kids who didn't want to learn.

"Then I looked at the kids. And in their faces I saw apathy and sadness where spirit and pride should be."

Basil paused. I think almost everybody was holding their breath, waiting to hear what came next.

"Well, I'd like to do something about these problems. I want to turn this school around. A long time ago, Mr. Hawthorne saved the students' lives in this school. I want to save the heart of this school now. Please give me your help to do that."

Even before Basil stopped talking, everybody was clapping. Kids were on their feet, shouting and roaring. I thought to myself that we didn't even need the election. Basil was in!

I was happy for Basil and happy for the school. But I was still feeling low about myself. Ms. Brundage had a big say in who won the scholarship. I could do well on the current affairs test, write a terrific essay, and lose anyway.

It made me furious to think I could lose the scholarship because she thought I was some kind of madwoman! It was so unfair.

That day after school, I was headed for my bike when a familiar voice stopped me. I turned and smiled at Basil. "You were great at the assembly today," I said. "You won everybody over."

"I hope so. You got a minute?"

"Sure."

"I understand the big social event of the

season here is the homecoming dance."

"Yeah."

"I suppose you've already lined up a date for it," he said.

I dropped my eyes in embarrassment. "Uh—no—not really."

"Well, then, would you go with me?"

I couldn't believe my ears. I stared at Basil, and before my eyes he turned into a black-caped knight. Instead of his sweater and blue jeans, he wore lace at his throat and shiny black boots.

"I'd love to," I finally managed to stammer.

"Great!" He smiled and waved as he rode off on his motorcycle. But, of course, it wasn't a motorcycle. It was a spirited, gleaming black horse.

As I started for home, I forgot all about Ms. Brundage and my problems. I felt great! I had a date with Basil Harris!

4 THAT EVENING I noticed that Dad looked worried. "Is everything okay at work?" I asked.

"Oh, sure. But they're talking about a short layoff." My mother quickly shifted the conversation to other topics.

I felt sorry for him and my mother. Though they both worked, they were always worrying about Dad being laid off or the house payments. I really *had* to win that school scholarship. I didn't want to add to their money worries.

So far I'd spent about two nights working on my essay. That night I went over it again. I tried to clearly state just why I felt being a teacher was so important. Then I listed on the application all the school activities I'd been involved in. I had to add an extra page to fit everything in.

The next day I let Basil read the essay. "It's very good," he said when he finished. "You have a flair for words."

"Thanks. But I still have to do well on the current affairs test."

"And I told you, I'm sure you will."

"And then—" I stopped, wondering how Basil would take the news. "Well, I have epilepsy. Ms. Brundage keeps hinting around that that's a big problem."

Basil stared at me. "Why should it be?"

I frowned. "Well, it shouldn't be. But some people think epileptics have mental or emotional problems. Ms. Brundage seems to be one of those. And she has a big say in who wins the scholarship."

Though I was unsure of my own chances, I knew that Basil was bound to win the school election. And sure enough, by the end of the election day, we got the good news. The principal, Ms. Baldwin, announced that Basil had won by a landslide.

The next day, Basil started right in on his school improvement program. He called a meeting of the student council and all interested students.

"The kids from the Spanish Club are

going to paint a mural on the outside wall of the gym," he told us.

"Who cares?" Jim Argus murmured.

He'd been forced to come to the meeting to turn over power to Basil.

"We do," a red-haired boy replied.

Everybody laughed and cheered. It was amazing. You could just see school spirit building.

"It will be great to see some nice murals on the walls instead of graffiti," Dina said.

Dennie, who'd turned up just to support Jim, laughed. "This is all kid stuff. Who really gives a damn about this school?"

Despite Jim's and Dennie's sour grapes, everyone felt pretty positive by the time the meeting broke up.

As most of the students filed out of the room, Jan went over to congratulate Basil. "I think your new plans are just great."

"Thanks."

Jan said something else then that I couldn't hear. I think she was hinting about the homecoming dance. Basil must have told her he was taking me because I heard her say my name in a surprised voice.

Later on Jan walked up to me while I was standing at my locker. "I hear you're going to the dance with Basil."

"Yeah, that's right."

"Well, congratulations. I'm awfully glad for you. Basil is so sweet. I mean, isn't it just like him to be taking you? It's such a nice gesture of gratitude toward you. Thanking you for being such a loyal little supporter."

I felt the hair on my neck begin to rise in anger. "Basil and I are friends. He doesn't owe me a thing."

"Oh, I'm sure Basil isn't one to forget a debt. He owes you that date, Valerie, and you have it coming to you." She gave me a nasty smile and I read the malice in her eyes. She couldn't accept the fact that Basil was taking me instead of her. She was hurt. So she wanted to hurt me, too. Well, I wasn't about to give her that satisfaction.

Jan aimed another blow at me. "You're taking the current affairs test on Monday, aren't you?"

"Yes."

"Evan Wasserman is taking it, too. He's

a real big brain. Tasha and Jason are taking it, too. They really know about current events. I'd be surprised if you beat them."

I wondered just how childish Jan would get before calling it quits.

"Well, I'm sure going to try."

"Hmm. Well, good luck." With that and one more fake smile, Jan glided off.

I decided to ignore Jan. There was so much happening at school, I didn't really have to fake it. Basil's school rebuilding plan took up a lot of my time. The very next day after school, I joined about thirty kids in whitewashing the walls.

After we were finished, the Spanish Club began the mural. Basil was in that club, and he was really good at painting.

I talked to Basil about the mural. He told me, "I want it to show life in America at the time the school was founded."

"Won't you have to do a lot of research? I mean to get the clothes and buildings right?" I asked him.

He smiled. "No. I told you how much I liked the nineteenth century. I already know a lot about it."

In the next few days, things really started getting better. The Ecology Club had a litter clean-up party. Then some of the science classes planted new shrubs and a bed of flowers.

Even some of the troublemakers started shaping up. Whenever Jim and Dennie would mess up in class, somebody would put them down fast.

It was like a miracle. We used to call Hawthorne "The Dump," but not anymore. Except for people like Jim and Dennie, most of the kids were really proud of what was happening.

* * *

That weekend I devoted a lot of my time to reviewing for the current events test. Both Mom and Dad helped by quizzing me over magazines I checked out from the library.

Monday after school, I sat with twenty-four other students taking the test. My stomach ached as I waited for the exams to be handed out. I wanted to win this scholarship so much.

I looked around at the other students.

Most looked just as nervous as I did. They were good kids and they all deserved to win. But I *had* to win.

At last they handed out the tests. There were a lot of questions on the Middle East. I had expected that and I knew the answers. There also was an outline map of Africa. I felt I got most of the nations right.

The next section covered Russia. I was less positive about my answers here. But I was very sure about the last two parts which covered the Americas and Europe.

I finished the test and reviewed my work until the teacher called for our papers. I felt pretty good about my answers. I knew I had done well. But I didn't know if I had done better than everybody else.

"Tough test, huh?" Evan said as we walked out together afterwards.

"Yeah," I said. "I think I did okay, though."

"I think I did okay, too." Evan smiled. "Too bad we both can't win, huh?"

"Yeah," I said. And I meant it.

"I want to teach biology, but my parents haven't got the money for college," Evan said.

"I know what you mean. I want to teach disabled kids."

We looked at each other with half grins on our faces. It was like being in a sinking boat with one life raft. We both needed it, but only one of us would fit.

"Good luck, Valerie," Evan said.

"Same to you, Evan."

* * *

For the rest of the week, I was too nervous to think about anything except the test. Then on Friday, they posted the test scores. My heart nearly stopped. Tasha had scored a 94 and Evan got a 96.

Then I saw my name. I had scored 100!

I couldn't believe it!

Mr. Prager saw me looking at the scores and came over. "I can't remember anybody ever scoring 100 on that test. Congratulations, Valerie," he said with a warm smile.

"Thanks!" I said, giving him a huge smile in return.

A bunch of kids, overheard this remark. They gathered around to congratulate me. Basil was there, too. He grinned and said, "Fantastic!"

Jan came up then. She looked at the score. I thought she was going to faint. "Well—that's great," she muttered.

"Thanks," I said.

Then she gathered her energy for the attack. "Isn't it a shame that such an intelligent person like you has to have that awful disease? I mean, you could have a really fine career if it weren't for that," she said.

This whole little speech was delivered in a loud voice. She obviously wanted Basil to hear her. I guess she hoped to scare Basil out of taking me to the dance.

"It must be terrible when you drool. Or pass out and fall down," Jan went on.

I glared at her. But just as I was about to say something, Basil turned. He coldly stared at Jan. "Ah, but your disease. Well, that's much worse, Jan."

"What do you mean?" she asked.

"It turns the skin green and makes the

eyes beady. I've heard it can even make people grow claws."

"What are you talking about?" Jan asked uneasily.

"Jealousy."

Jan tried to laugh it off. "Jealousy? You must be crazy—"

"You're angry because I didn't want to take you to the dance. You're not used to guys turning you down, Jan. Well, I'm sorry, but I wouldn't take a girl like you anywhere. You're too shallow and conceited."

Jan stepped back as if she'd been slapped. Then she turned and hurried away.

I just stood there, sort of shocked. Then a smile crept across my face. I had to admit that I enjoyed seeing Jan get a little cold water thrown at her.

When I got home that day, I told my parents about scoring 100 on the test. They were really proud and happy. Like me, they felt that my chances for getting the scholarship were really good now.

At school the next morning, my high

spirits were quickly lowered. As I walked towards the building, I saw a crowd of kids standing by the mural. When I got closer, I saw why. The whole thing had been splashed with purple paint.

My heart sank. "Who did it?" I asked Dina, who was also there.

"Some lousy vandals," Dina said. Her voice was hard and bitter. "And we all worked so hard!"

"They threw paint at the statue, too," a boy said.

I hurried over to the statue. I could remember staring at that statue in fascination ever since I was a little girl. Once, when I was about eight, I asked my dad about the "bronze man." He told me the whole heroic story. Now I stared sadly at Mr. Hawthorne's paint-streaked figure.

"A lovely way to start a day, huh?" Basil said as he came up beside me.

"It makes me sick. I wonder who did it?"

"They're investigating. But it's obvious it was somebody who's mad about the changes at school. Undoubtedly they liked 'The Dump' better." Basil seemed really angry.

"I'm so sorry, Basil."

"I know. We all are. Except for the ones who did it."

"Have you heard any names being mentioned? Sometimes the kids sort of know who does stuff like this," I said.

"Yes, I know who's responsible," Basil said simply.

I stared at him. "You *know*? Have you told the principal?"

"No. I don't have proof. I just know. I think it's best that I handle it myself." Basil smiled in that strange way of his.

"Look, Basil," I said quickly. "I don't believe in taking things like that into your own hands. You could get hurt—"

He went on smiling. "It's all right, Valerie. It really is. Believe me."

For once Basil failed to convince me. I was still afraid he was going to take the law into his own hands.

Then I remembered Bob and Dennie. Suddenly I wondered who I should be more frightened for—Basil or the vandals.

5 THE VANDALS DIDN'T hide themselves for long. In English class that day, Jim and Dennie all but shouted they were responsible.

When I walked in the room, they were grinning and shoving each other. Then Dennie spotted me. He called out, "You guys are really doing a great job on the mural. I like the purple paint. Was that your idea?"

I glared at Dennie. "Were you the one who messed up the mural?"

He laughed. "Oh, you mean it isn't supposed to look like that?"

Jim laughed, too. "I like it better with the purple paint."

The conversation was interrupted when Mr. Prager stepped into the room. Not even Jim and Dennie wanted to risk being caught for vandalism by a teacher.

Mr. Prager called roll. Then he announced, "Your papers on symbolism are due today."

As everybody pulled out folders, Mr. Prager went down the rows collecting the papers. When he got to Jim, he stopped.

"Where's your paper, Jim?"

With a wise guy grin, Jim opened his folder. "Right here." He paused, then exclaimed, "Hey, wait a minute! It's gone!"

Mr. Prager frowned. "Don't give me that. You forgot to do the paper, that's all."

"But I did do it!" Jim was almost shouting. He began to wildly dig through his binder. I really believed him. He lied and made excuses a lot. But this time he seemed to be telling the truth.

"Come on, Argus," another boy whispered as Mr. Prager passed by. "You didn't do that paper and everybody knows it!"

Mr. Prager continued down the rows until he came to Dennie. Dennie didn't have his paper either. "I had it right here," he said. "I swear I had it right here!"

"Perhaps there's a paper-eating monster on the loose," Mr. Prager said dryly.

Everybody laughed except Jim and Dennie.

After class was over, the two boys walked out of class together. "Somebody stole my paper," Jim stormed.

"Mine, too," Dennie said. "But who? And how?"

Jim's eyes narrowed to slits. "I'll bet it was Harris. He must be the one behind this."

"Yeah," Dennie agreed quickly. "There's something weird about him. He made me choke. Man, he's some kind of freak!"

"I wonder how that freak would like to get his head busted," Jim said.

When I saw Basil that day, I told him what I'd heard. "You better be careful, Basil. Those guys really think you took their papers."

Basil smiled. "Why would I do such a thing? I'm not a vengeful person. I know they messed up the mural. But why should I want to make trouble for them over that?"

I stared at Basil. "You did have something to do with them losing their papers, didn't you?"

"Valerie, suppose I *could* make them believe they can't get away with causing trouble? What would be so terrible about that?"

Basil gave another of his dazzling smiles. Then he walked over to the mural. A group of kids were busily repainting there. Already a lot of the damage had been repaired.

Ms. Baldwin, the principal, came over to admire the work. "Excellent detail. Everything seems so accurate," she commented.

"Basil designed it," I said.

The principal smiled at Basil. "Great job. You have all sorts of talents. I've been hearing marvelous things about you from all the teachers. Praises for your fine singing voice, your artistic skill, your leadership abilities. You really have taken this school by storm. Tell me, Basil, what are your plans after graduation?"

Basil got a strange look on his face. "Oh, I don't know. I try to take each day as it comes."

The conversation got me thinking.

Basil never seemed to want to talk about his future or his past. It was funny, but it almost seemed like he had no past and no future. He seemed to exist only in the present.

Later I told Dina what I'd observed about Basil. Dina got a wicked smile on her face. "But didn't you know? He's the crown prince of Banari," she teased me. "He's just here at Hawthorne to try life among the common people."

"Oh, Dina!" I laughed.

"Okay, okay. The truth: he's the son of the famous jazz musician Roland Harris."

"Of course. And you're Cleopatra's daughter!"

"But seriously," Dina said, "there really is something mysterious and romantic about him. For instance, did you ever see that beautiful gold watch of his? It has the initials 'B. H.' engraved on it. It looks really expensive—and old. I've never seen a watch with a chain outside a museum. I bet it's been in his family for years."

"I bet he has a very sad past," I said. "That's why he doesn't want to talk about it. His parents must have died young. So now he thinks life is short and you shouldn't make plans."

"And you thought my ideas were wild and romantic!" Dina exclaimed. We both laughed.

Then Dina snapped her fingers. "I forgot to tell you the latest. Did you hear about what happened to Jim and Dennie?"

"You mean about them losing their papers?" I asked.

"No, more recent than that. When they went out for lunch break, they tried to start their cars. And guess what? They were both out of gas!"

Basil again? I couldn't be sure. But if it was, it seemed to me that he was getting in over his head. Jim and Dennie could really be mean.

By the end of the next day, all traces of purple paint were gone from the mural. But a specialist would have to fix the statue of Mr. Hawthorne. The bronze had to be carefully cleaned.

After school that day as I was walking to my bike, I saw Basil with Jim and Dennie. Jim was saying, "We got a pretty good idea who stole our papers."

Dennie added, "Yeah, and who drained our gas tanks!"

"Really?" Basil said. He sounded very calm.

"Yeah," Jim snarled. "And if you don't want a nasty accident of your own, you'll quit messing with us."

"And I would suggest that if retribution isn't to your liking, you stop your vandalism." Basil gave them an icy smile.

"Retrib—what's that supposed to mean?" Dennie asked.

"Retribution? Punishment for evil deeds," Basil said.

Both Jim and Dennie glared at that and stepped closer to Basil. I knew there was going to be a fight. They both looked mad enough to kill somebody. But the principal came along just then. Jim and Dennie went their way, and Basil came over to me.

"I'm scared, Basil," I said.

"Scared of what?"

"You don't know how tough those guys can be."

He laughed. "They can't hurt me,

Valerie. Don't worry. Now let's forget all about them and talk about something else. And somewhere else. Let's go to the little cafe on Crawford and get a drink."

So we did. I got on the back of his motorcycle, and we drove down to the cafe. As we sat sipping our sodas, Basil asked about my family. Gradually I worked my way around to talking about his family, too. I asked him if he minded living with his grandmother.

"Isn't she pretty old? I'll bet she's old-fashioned."

"In many ways she's younger than I am," he replied. "You ought to meet Faith. You'd love her, Valerie. And I know she'd love you."

"Faith? Is that her name?"

"Yes."

"Well, I'd love to meet her, Basil."

"How about today? I can take you there on my motorcycle. Then I'll drop you back at school so you can pick up your bike."

"Today?" I considered. "Okay, I'd like that."

We were at Basil's house in just a few

minutes. It was a tiny frame house with big window boxes painted blue. They were filled with flowers.

Faith was in the front yard. She was a small woman with huge, warm eyes. She looked like a picture from a child's storybook.

When Faith saw me, she gave me a big smile. "You must be Valerie. Basil has told me about you."

"Hello," I said. "It's a pleasure meeting you—"

"Faith, please call me Faith." She clasped my hands with her own soft, wrinkled ones. Then she said, "Do come in the house. I have some cider and anise cookies ready. I made them fresh."

Basil interrupted. "I'll join you two ladies in a moment. I promised to feed the Dawsons' cat while they're out of town."

Faith bowed her head as gracefully as a queen. "You're excused."

As we walked to the house, Faith gave me another long glance. "Basil told me how sweet and intelligent you are. But he didn't say how pretty you are."

I smiled in reply, too embarrassed to speak.

The house was cool and tidy inside. Many paintings hung on the walls. Tiny china figurines stood on the tables. I settled on a couch in what Faith called her "sitting room" while she got the "refreshments."

Faith soon appeared with a full tray. She poured me some cider from a lovely cut-glass pitcher. Then she passed a plate of tiny cookies, shiny with sugar.

"These cookies are wonderful," I exclaimed as I took a bite.

"It's a special family recipe. Oh, here's Basil."

He came through the doorway. "The cat is fed, and now it's my turn," he declared. His eyes were sparkling.

"Everything is so pretty here," I said to Basil. "It's such an interesting house."

"And quite ancient," Faith said. "Like me."

Somehow I felt that Basil belonged in this quaint house. It suited him. Yes, he wore work shirts and faded jeans. And he rode a motorcycle. Yet none of that quite seemed right for him. This seemed his proper place—this strange, beautiful, storybook house.

I looked at Basil as he stood there. Without a doubt, he was the most fascinating boy I'd ever met.

But something about Basil made me uneasy. Always at the back of my mind was the fear that he wouldn't be around for long. Like a candle slowly burning away, he would offer me his warm light only for a short time.

6 ON MONDAY THE class valedictorian was announced. It was Evan Wasserman. The salutatorian was Tasha Phillips.

All three of us had the same grade point average, so I'd thought I might be given one of the positions. I wasn't too disappointed though. But after Dina heard the announcement, she said, "I'll bet Ms. Brundage saw to it you weren't named!"

"Maybe not, Dina. Anyway, I don't care that much. And Evan is a good speaker."

Dina shook her head. "Someone told me they heard Brundage talking to another teacher about the selection for class speakers. Brundage was saying she thought it would be 'wisest' if you weren't 'put under that strain.'"

I got very tense. "Are you sure that's what she said?"

"Well, I didn't hear it. But it sounds like Brundage, doesn't it?" Dina frowned. "I think you should protest!"

"Oh, Dina, I can't. Everybody'd just say I was a sore loser," I said.

"But what if Brundage kills the scholarship, too?" Dina said.

My heart sank. I figured I had better talk to the principal. I had to make Ms. Baldwin understand.

The next free period I had, I went to Ms. Baldwin's office. After she had finished seeing another student, I nervously entered her room.

"Ms. Baldwin. May I see you?"

"Of course. Valerie Moran, isn't it? Please sit down."

I took a seat and began, though I had to fight my shaking voice. "Ms. Baldwin, I don't want to sound like a poor loser because I don't care that much about being valedictorian. But somebody told me I wasn't even considered because I have epilepsy."

Ms. Baldwin pushed her chair back. She looked at me in surprise. "Well, I don't think your information is correct, Valerie. I know the selection process for valedictorian was tough this year. You must realize that we had to consider grades, activities, citizenship, and teacher recommendations."

Teacher recommendations. Just what kind of recommendation would Ms. Brundage have given me?

"I realize it was a tough decision, Ms. Baldwin," I said. "I just don't want the fact that I have epilepsy to ever count against me. You see, I'm up for a scholarship, too. I'm afraid I'll lose it because people think I'm mentally ill or something."

That really seemed to make Ms. Baldwin nervous. At last she said, "I don't think there's any reason for you to worry, Valerie. I'm sure the issue will be decided on merit alone."

"That's fine," I said as I got up to leave. "As long as my epilepsy isn't considered a *de*-merit."

There was nothing else to say. At least not on my part. But as I headed out into the hall, I heard the principal speaking in a low voice to her secretary.

I wasn't convinced that Ms. Baldwin really believed me—or even cared. I felt like one of those poor rats in a maze. I was trapped by the stupid walls people kept putting up when they heard the word "epilepsy." I wondered if there was anyone on the faculty who would take my side.

Suddenly I thought of Mrs. Gottsman. I hurried to the music room. I found her there playing the piano.

"Sounds lovely, Mrs. Gottsman," I said after she drifted to a close.

She looked up and smiled. "Ah, not so good now. The arthritis in the fingers—" She laughed. "So, Valerie, what can I do for you?"

"Are you busy now?"

"Busy? You are my student. For you, I have time. Come—sit down."

It was the first time I'd ever really talked to Mrs. Gottsman. I saw things about her I'd never seen before. For one thing, she had beautiful brown eyes and a surprisingly sweet face. Always before I'd just seen the wrinkles.

As we talked, I was also surprised

to find how easy it was to tell her my worries. I told her everything.

After I finished, Mrs. Gottsman said, "Prejudice—it is a tricky thing, Valerie. Sometimes it hides so cleverly, we do not even see it inside ourselves. But you must also beware of suspecting the innocent. That can become a kind of prejudice, too. Do you see?"

I nodded thoughfully. Then Mrs. Gottsman patted my hand. "But enough of the lecture. Listen, Valerie. I have known Ms. Baldwin for years. I think she would treat you fairly. And remember, too, I am on the scholarship committee. So try not to worry."

Then she winked at me. "In fact, we have already read your essay. It's one of the best we've received."

I almost cried from relief. At last the odds seem to be turning in my favor. I thanked Mrs. Gottsman and went to my next class feeling much calmer.

After school I rode home on Basil's motorcycle. "Want to hear something funny?" I said to him as we sped along.

"I don't think you really belong on a motorcycle. I picture you more as the shiny-black-horse type."

He laughed. "As a matter of fact, I have ridden some shiny black horses."

"Really? And I bet you've ridden in a carriage, too." I was just kidding him.

"If you count a handsome buggy," he said.

I peered at his face and caught his usual mysterious smile. Did he want me to take him seriously or not? I couldn't decide, so I merely said, "You like old things, don't you?"

"I guess so. I like a lot of things. Dancing with lovely women included. Speaking of which, are you ready for the dance on Saturday?"

"All set," I assured him. But I didn't tell him I had to get my hair cut and styled yet. Nor did I tell him I'd bought a new dress for the dance. I would have felt foolish talking about how special this date was to me—or how special he himself was.

He hesitated for a moment. Then he gently said, "Val, I was disappointed that you weren't selected valedictorian."

"Yeah. Well, Ms. Brundage might have had something to do with that. Anyway, I'm more concerned about the scholarship. I just don't want Ms. Brundage to ruin my chances for that. I talked to Mrs. Gottsman today about it. She says I have a good chance."

"Mrs. Gottsman is a caring person," Basil commented.

"Did you know that she lost her whole family in concentration camps during the war?"

"Caring and brave to live through that. How can people be so cruel?" Basil said.

"Yeah." It saddened me to think how much pain and loss Mrs. Gottsman had suffered. "But you're right, Basil. She's really got a lot of courage. She came through all that, and she still wants to help people."

"That's what life is all about," Basil said, "helping people. That's what we're here for." He pulled up in front of my house and dropped me off. "I'll pick you up at seven tomorrow," he called. With a wave, he took off.

I thought about what Basil had said. He really didn't have to convince me how important helping others was. That's what I intended to do all along. The scholarship was my chance at getting the training to do a good job of it.

I thought I might have some talent for teaching, too. At least I was getting my feet wet by doing volunteer work once a week at a center for the disabled. The staff there seemed to think I did my job right. In fact, they were considering me for a job with pay next semester.

That pleased me. The job would really help me out. Even with the scholarship, I would still need money for college.

And I really loved the little kids. They needed a lot of love. I guess I had a little more patience than most people, so the kids didn't get me down.

I dropped by the center the next day to talk to the director, Ms. Ahlgren, about the job. I was overjoyed when she said, "Valerie, we've looked over the candidates for our part-time openings. Everyone has agreed that we should hire you."

She smiled when I eagerly thanked her. "You're a special one," Ms. Ahlgren told me, "a caring person. That's why we want you here."

She handed me the employee forms, and I walked out of the center on a cloud. I was so happy that the idea of getting my hair cut no longer made me nervous. I sat down in the chair at the hair salon. It seemed only a few minutes later my hair was done.

I studied my reflection for a moment. I decided I liked it. I hoped Basil would, too.

That night at seven o'clock sharp, Basil drove up in a nice little sports car. "Is this yours?" I asked him.

"No. I wanted to bring the carriage. But I borrowed this instead." He abruptly stopped talking and gazed at me. "You look exquisite," he said.

I smiled. I'd hoped that I looked pretty. But I'd never heard a guy call me "exquisite." In fact, I'd never heard the word used at all, except in movies!

As we drove to the dance, I gazed

happily out the window. The night was perfect. Tiny stars glowed and twinkled everywhere.

"What a pretty night. And all those stars! They look like millions of fireflies," I said.

"They do at that," Basil agreed. "I remember some beautiful summer evenings in Ohio. You could hardly tell the fireflies from the stars."

"Are you from Ohio?"

"Yes. A farm there."

I smiled. "You don't seem like a farm boy."

"And just what does a farm boy seem like?" he teased. "But those were fine days, Valerie. I can still see those fields of corn. They grew so high, they seemed to scratch the clouds.

"And the cows—huge black-and-white cows. Just like salt and pepper sprinkled across the fields. One of my chores was milking them. I think I could still do it in my sleep. Ah, but the rewards—have you ever tasted fresh ice cream, Valerie?"

"You made ice cream by hand?" I asked.

"Sure. Blueberry ice cream from our

own blueberries. And we drank water from the stream."

"A stream? You mean it was clean enough to drink?"

"Yes. And sweet, too," he said with a fond smile.

We reached the school and parked. There were a lot of cars there already.

As we entered the gym, we stopped and and took in the decorations. The room was strung with red and black streamers in keeping with the school colors. From the rafters hung papier-mâché footballs. At the north and south ends of the gym stood cardboard goal posts.

"Dina was head of the decorations committee," I told Basil. "Didn't she do a great job?"

"Great," he said.

"I've never seen so many kids at a dance. I know everyone is happy about the fact that we won the game last night. But I think we're all more in a mood to celebrate because of the changes at Hawthorne. Thanks to you, Basil."

Basil shook his head. "Thanks to

everybody who helped out."

In a far corner of the room, I saw Dennie and Jim and Jan. Jan had taken up with them again. I wished they hadn't come at all. They usually did their best to ruin things.

Basil led me out onto the floor as soon as the band started up. He proved to be a wonderful dancer. He even did the new dances perfectly, though he said he didn't like them much.

"I'd rather hold a girl close in my arms," he said.

"Did your parents dance like that?" I asked.

"Oh, yes. They loved the waltz. Though sometimes they square-danced."

I longed to find out more about his parents. However, I didn't want to make him sad. So I decided not to ask any more questions.

As we turned, I saw Jan by the punch bowl. She had taken a bottle out of a paper sack and was starting to open it. Basil saw her, too. He stopped dancing and walked over to Jan. She saw him coming and hurriedly put the bottle back in the sack.

"What's in the bottle?" he asked her.

"What bottle?" Jan asked, pretending she didn't know what he was talking about.

"The bottle in that sack. The one you tried to dump into the punch bowl." Basil's voice was hard.

"You're a regular saint, aren't you, Basil Harris?" Jan said bitterly. "And about as much fun as a dead dog. Look, I was just trying to give this stupid dance a little life."

"Some of the kids don't want to drink, Jan. Why not leave the choice up to them?" Basil said.

"Mr. Clean to the rescue!" she said with an angry laugh.

"Give me the bottle, Jan," Basil said.

"Go to hell, boy scout!" Jan snapped.

"Do you want me to tell the chaperone you brought liquor in here?" Basil asked.

"You'd get me in trouble?" Jan stared at him.

In icy silence, Basil stared back at her.

"Yeah, you would," Jan bitterly concluded. "Someday you're going to butt in too far, Harris! So far you'll never climb out." Her voice was ugly and hate-filled. But she gave Basil the bottle.

Basil took the bottle and dumped it out in the bathroom. Then he rejoined me as though nothing had happened. But as we slowly spun around the dance floor, I caught a glimpse of Jan talking to Jim and Dennie. Their faces were fixed in scowls and frowns, and they were staring straight at Basil. They seemed to be plotting something.

I knew what they were planning. One way or another, they were going to get back at Basil.

7 AS MUCH AS the sight of the scheming troublemakers bothered me, I forgot about them after a while. It was so much fun being with Basil that the dance ended all too soon. On the way home we stopped to get something to eat. I suggested we go to a little coffee house. We settled into a cozy corner booth and talked as we shared a pizza.

At one point, I stopped and listened to some music playing in the background. It was soft, but the words drew my attention.

Answer me a riddle, if you please,
why nobody cares for the quiet man
who softly walks through life just
doing the best that he can?

His fine friends are no friends at all,
saying what's good and what's best,
when all they mean is "He's not right,"
and "That's just a fool's quest."

But the quiet man, he doesn't listen.
His way is to fix and to mend,

and then pass on when the job is done,
Alone, quite alone, in the end.

Basil was silent for a moment after the song ended. Then he looked at me. "Nobody is alone," he declared. "There are friends and good spirits everywhere."

I smiled. "Spirits?"

"Yes. I mean the voices—or the ideas and feelings—of the dead. The souls of those who will never abandon a noble cause."

I decided Basil was using more of his poetic language. So I didn't press him further.

We talked for a while longer. Then Basil drove me home. Before I got out of the car, he said, "Valerie, may I kiss you?"

I couldn't believe he asked. A guy either didn't even try or just kissed you without asking. I smiled at him and said, "I'd like that."

Basil leaned closer and gave me a long, tender kiss.

It was a magical thing. I suddenly felt like a fine lady who'd just been swept off her feet by a caped man of mystery.

Still in a lovely fog, I walked to the door with Basil. He again brushed my lips. Then he softly said good night.

When I walked into the house, I found my parents in the living room. They were watching an old movie on TV. I told them I'd had a great time, and they both smiled.

But I knew something was wrong. Dad looked really bad.

"Did something happen at work?" I asked him.

He tried to smile bravely. "Sorry to spoil your evening, honey, but I guess there's no putting it off. I was laid off today."

Mom saw my look of concern. "I'm sure everything will be okay, Valerie. We've still got our savings, and my job is safe."

"Maybe I'll try another kind of work," Dad said. "I'm sick of driving a truck. I'm even sicker of being laid off every time business is slow."

"You have a good personality, Dad," I said. "You'd make a terrific salesman."

But in my heart, I didn't have much hope for the idea. Dad was fifty-three. Most companies don't like to hire someone that age.

"I could sell real estate maybe," Dad said. "They say there's money in that."

"That's a good idea," I said.

I went to bed feeling depressed. I knew my parents worried about all the bills. We had a big mortgage and car payments. I would be working next semester, but that wouldn't help much. What would happen if Dad were off work for a long time? We couldn't live off just Mom's salary.

All during the next week, Dad looked for a job. Everywhere it was the same story. He was given applications to fill out, but no one hired him. Of course they tried to hide the real reason, but my father knew. They wanted someone younger.

Dad's spirits sank lower and lower. I overheard him talking to Mom one night in the kitchen. They thought I'd already gone to bed.

"Maybe if you changed your age a little bit," Mom said. "You know, on the applications. Maybe it's not right, but—"

"Don't you think I haven't done that?" Dad said in a sad voice. "I said I was five years younger than I am. They still don't want me."

"Oh." Mom's voice was very small.

"I don't know what to do," Dad said. "I've tried everything. Nothing seems to work."

Tears filled my eyes. I felt so sorry for Dad. It just wasn't fair.

Then on Saturday morning, Dad came home whistling. I tore down the stairs and found Mom already at the door. We stared as Dad entered the house with a brand new cap on his head. On the front in red letters was printed "Fleet Cab Company."

"So that's what the mystery job interview was!" Mom exclaimed. "And they hired you?"

Dad tipped his hat and smiled. "They sure did, honey."

"But is it what you want?" she asked. "I mean, I know you hoped to get out of the truck driving business—"

"It's good, clean work. Plus it's a lot easier than driving a truck. And since I know every street in the city, this will work out just fine. I think it's a good company, too. They were really nice to me. I feel at home already."

I could see from Dad's face that the job meant even more than the money. He needed to be doing something. He'd felt so useless.

Mom saw that, too. She gave Dad a big hug and kiss. "Well, I can't imagine they'll have a nicer driver in the whole company."

"Lady, you give one fine tip," Dad said with a smile. He added with a more serious look, "The money won't be as good as with my old company. But we'll manage."

"I'm almost sure I'll get the scholarship, Dad," I said. "So you won't have to worry about my college."

Dad smiled at me. "Let's keep our fingers crossed, honey."

In just another few weeks, I would know for sure about the scholarship. I tried to think of other things, and my dates with Basil were a lovely distraction. But I couldn't stop worrying. This scholarship was so important to me.

I did the best I could in all my classes. I wanted to show my teachers I was more serious than ever about my studies.

I worked especially hard on my English term paper. I knew Mr. Prager was one of the teachers on the scholarship committee. As I sat in the library one day doing some research for it, Basil came over.

"How's it coming?" he asked me.

"Okay. I've decided to concentrate on religion in English poetry. I have a lot on William Blake and Alfred Lord Tennyson. But I need some others," I said.

"What about George Herbert?" Basil suggested.

We looked in the card catalog. To my disappointment, I found that there were no books on Herbert.

"Don't worry," Basil said. "I have two books at home you can use."

The next day Basil brought me two ancient-looking books. "Where on earth did you get these?" I asked him.

"Oh, from the family collection," he smiled. "They were gifts to me from my parents. Herbert was my father's favorite poet."

I opened the book and skimmed the first pages. "Published in 1884!" I exclaimed. "Basil, are you sure you want to trust these to me? I mean, they must be valuable."

"Please, I wish you would use them. I think they'll give your paper a special magic." Basil sounded so serious. I wasn't sure how to interpret his word "magic."

I did use the two books and they were perfect. They were just what my paper had needed. I felt really good about my rough draft when I turned it in.

But a few days later when Mr. Prager began handing the papers back, I felt my heart sink. He pulled out the stack and scowled at us. "Most of you did terrible jobs!" he complained. He stalked up and down the aisles, slapping the papers down on our desks.

"It's hard for me to believe you people are in high school," he coldly stated. "You write like second graders!"

Now I was really scared. Maybe I hadn't done such a good job after all!

Mr. Prager paused at Dennie's desk and

tossed a paper down. "Dennis, unless you want an F for plagiarism, I'd better see another rough draft fast. This is almost a word-for-word copy of an encyclopedia article."

Mr. Prager seemed disgusted with all of us.

Then he reached my desk. He stopped and said softly, "Valerie, yours is the only good paper in the bunch."

I felt like leaping into the air and screaming for joy.

Then I remembered Basil's words about there being magic in those old books. There certainly had been for me.

I took my rough draft home and began work. I was determined to make my final paper outstanding.

In the next week, almost all my free time was devoted to studying or working at the center for the disabled. Though I was working hard, I felt charged with energy. I really didn't mind being so busy.

But one day as I was rushing down the the hall, Ms. Brundage stopped me. "Valerie, you look tired," she said.

"Oh, I'm not. I feel fine," I said.

"Well, you know you shouldn't overdo it," Ms. Brundage said. "You of all people should be careful about your health."

I guess she meant well, but I felt angry anyway. "Look, Ms. Brundage, I'm perfectly fine. And I wish you'd stop hinting that I'm going to bring on a fit if I overwork," I said angrily.

I continued. "Maybe it's time you learned a little bit about epilepsy, Ms. Brundage. In most cases—mine included—medication takes care of the condition very nicely. Julius Caesar and Peter the Great of Russia were epileptics, you know. And they did okay, don't you think? I mean, really, Ms. Brundage, both of them did a lot of important things. Maybe I might, too, if people like you would give me half a chance!"

Ms. Brundage drew back, a shocked look on her face. I guess she thought I was crazy or something.

I didn't wait for her to reply. I simply walked off. But even as I turned away, a sick feeling went through me. I knew it as surely as if someone had just whispered in my ear. I'd just blown my scholarship.

8 ON MONDAY IN music class, Mrs. Gottsman announced, "Today we'll start practicing for the holiday assembly. Some of you have already signed up to volunteer for songs or parts. I'd like to begin with a few Hanukkah songs that George volunteered to teach us. George, would you sing the songs now?"

George Walsh handed Mrs. Gottsman some sheet music. Then he stood by the piano and ran through one of the songs in his nice baritone voice.

It was beautiful, and all the kids were eager to learn it. That is, all except Dennie.

"What a stupid song," Dennie mumbled. "Why is that old bat trying to shove it down our throats?"

"I like it," I said.

Another girl who overheard Dennie's remark said, "I like it, too. Face it, Plover, you've got a tin ear."

Dennie slumped back in his chair, a fierce scowl on his face. He looked really mean today. I could tell he was just aching to cause trouble.

Suddenly he said, "Hey, Mrs. Gottsman, how about a little Wagner for the program? I bet some Wagner would really get everybody in the holiday mood."

For a minute, Mrs. Gottsman stood there staring at Dennie. Then I noticed her hands were shaking. What was it? Why was she so upset?

Then I remembered something I'd read in a history book. Richard Wagner had been Hitler's favorite musician. I realized at once that Dennie must have found that out. He'd brought up the subject just to hurt Mrs. Gottsman. I was so mad I could have punched him.

A boy finally said, "Wagner? Isn't he that opera guy? Man, I can't sing opera."

Everybody laughed. I hoped that would be the end of it. But Dennie wasn't ready to quit. It was like some evil force was inside him. He had to keep on saying vicious things.

"Did you ever go to a Wagnerian festival, Mrs. Gottsman?"

Mrs. Gottsman ignored him. "George, let's hear your second song."

But Dennie refused to shut up. "Some people think that Wagner was the world's greatest composer. My dad says it isn't fair that we can't listen to Wagner just because of you, Mrs. Gottsman."

"I will not have any more of this," Mrs. Gottsman said.

"Knock it off," Basil said. I'd never seen such anger on his face.

"People like you have too much power in this country," Dennie said. "Like, right now, you're forcing us to sing these stupid songs just because—"

"That is enough!" Mrs. Gottsman shouted. "I want you to leave my classroom at once, Dennis!"

"Why?" Dennie shouted back. "You've got no right to make me leave! Look, my parents pay taxes. So this isn't your classroom. It's my classroom."

"You'd better get out of here right now," Basil said in a low voice.

"You know where you can go, Harris?" Dennie hissed.

"Leave this room and don't return," Mrs. Gottsman said. "Either leave now or I will have you thrown out."

Dennie stood up slowly. He looked around and laughed. "You want me to leave? Well, maybe we *all* should leave. Come on, who else wants out of here?" He waited confidently by the door.

I waited, too, not sure what would happen. I knew that Dennie used to have a lot of followers at Hawthorne. He could always depend on plenty of kids to laugh along with him.

But our school had changed—thanks in large part to Basil. I hoped that the kids had finally seen Dennie for what he was—a troublemaking bully.

A half a minute passed. Then I realized no one was going to stand up. Most of the kids just sat there, quietly staring at Dennie.

Finally one of Dennie's friends said, "Go on, Dennie. You'll just get into more trouble if you stay."

"Pick up your books and leave," Mrs. Gottsman said. Her voice was still angry but now firmer.

Dennie glared at Mrs. Gottsman, but he picked up his books. It was obvious he was more than a little shaken. He hadn't expected this to happen. He'd thought it would be like old times at Hawthorne— Dennie Plover, the clown, breaking up another class. But everything had gone wrong.

"I'll be back," he said. "Don't you worry!" He slammed the door as he left.

After he was out of the room, Mrs. Gottsman slowly sat down. She was still trembling slightly. I could see that the incident had taken a lot out of her.

Basil saw it, too, because he quietly got up and moved to the piano. "I guess it's my turn to play, today. Ready when you are, George."

Mrs. Gottsman gave Basil a grateful smile.

After that, the class went well. Yet no one was about to forget what had happened. When the bell rang and the class filed out, everyone was talking about the incident.

Basil and I discussed it, too. "I can't

believe that even Dennie would stoop that low!" I exclaimed. "He's such a jerk!"

Basil nodded grimly. "He must hate himself to hate other people so much."

By lunch, news of what had happened was all over school. I was glad to hear most of the kids siding with Mrs. Gottsman. It seemed like we were all sick of Dennie Plover's cruel jokes.

Next day we heard that Dennie had been officially kicked out of music class. Nobody was much surprised except Dennie. He couldn't believe the trouble he was in. Ms. Baldwin had even told his parents that if Dennie caused any more trouble, he'd be suspended.

Dennie was really mad. He went all around the school telling lies about Mrs. Gottsman. He said she was too old to teach and that she'd lost her mind. He also kept claiming that Mrs. Gottsman had picked on him unfairly.

I finally got fed up with it. "Listen," I told Dennie, "stop lying about Mrs. Gottsman. You know you got just what you deserved when she kicked you out."

"Got what I deserved? What I deserve is an apology. Old Gottsman is crazy," Dennie said.

"Come on, Dennie. Grow up! Mrs. Gottsman isn't that bad. In fact, she's a really nice lady."

That set Dennie off again. He began calling Mrs. Gottsman some really obscene names. I got so mad, I did something I've never done to anybody before. I slapped Dennie right in the face!

I guess he would have hit me back, but there were too many kids around. I didn't wait around long for him to get up his courage. I turned and went into the library.

About five minutes later, Dina hurried into the library and came over to me. "I heard you slapped Plover!"

"Well, it didn't take very long for that little piece of news to spread. Yeah, Dina, I hit him. I guess I lost my temper."

"Oh, man, Valerie. I wish I could have been there!" Dina loved a good fight.

I felt sort of guilty though. Violence doesn't settle anything—even with somebody like Dennie. But it had made me furious when he said such awful things about Mrs. Gottsman.

The next morning at school, the first person I saw was Basil. I could see from his face that something was wrong.

"What is it?" I asked.

"It's Mrs. Gottsman. She's in the hospital," he said.

"Oh, no! What's wrong?"

"I went into the music class early this morning to bring her some sheet music she'd wanted. I found her lying on the floor, unconscious." Basil's eyes were on fire. I could tell from his face that there was more to this than a simple fainting spell.

"Somebody got into the music room last night," Basil continued. "Whoever it was pasted some Nazi posters all over the walls. They painted some swastikas, too. And they'd rigged a tape of one of Hitler's speeches. When Mrs. Gottsman opened the door, it was going full blast. It was still running when I got there."

Basil angrily shook his head. "The shock

was just too much for her. She has a bad heart, you know. She just collapsed."

"Basil—" I whispered. I couldn't believe anyone would pull such a mean trick on poor Mrs. Gottsman.

"Any other teacher might have yelled and torn the stuff off the walls. But Mrs. Gottsman suffered so much during the war. All the sadness came back to her. It was just too much. She's in the hospital now."

"Dennie must have done it," I said.

"I don't think so," Basil said. "They're investigating right now. I bet they'll find that Dennie spent the whole night in bed. He got somebody else to do his dirty work for him."

Gloom hung over the school that morning. We got a get-well card for Mrs. Gottsman and everybody signed it. We wanted to go to the hospital and visit her, but she was in intensive care. No visitors were allowed.

I felt terrible about Mrs. Gottsman. And I couldn't help having some selfish thoughts. Now Mrs. Gottsman wouldn't be on the scholarship committee. I'd heard that Ms. Holman would replace her. Ms. Holman and Ms. Brundage were good friends. I knew that my chance for the scholarship were now next to nothing.

When I got home from school, I told my parents what had happened. When I finished, I asked, "How can people be so cruel to somebody like Mrs. Gottsman?"

Dad said, "Some people are just twisted up in inside. They hate the whole world. But most of all, they hate themselves."

I stared at my dad. Besides loving him for being my father, I'd always thought he was pretty smart. He may never have made a lot of money, but he was smart in more important ways. For example, he really understood people.

"Basil said almost the same thing, Dad. You know, he's always saying things that make me stop and think. In so many ways he seems a lot older than other guys his age. In fact, he's the second smartest guy I know. You're the first, of course."

Dad grinned and gave me a mock salute. As he lifted his arm, his sweatshirt rolled back. I saw a long bandage wrapped around his arm.

"What happened, Dad?" I asked him, looking at the bandage.

"Oh, that. I was doing some woodwork in the garage. A stack of boards fell on my arm."

Dad tried to keep his voice casual. But I could tell from his eyes that he wasn't telling me the truth. I shook my head. "It happened on the job, didn't it?"

Dad took a deep breath. "Yeah, honey, it did. I guess I'm not much of a liar. I told your mother the same story, and she caught me out immediately."

"So what happened, Dad?"

"It's nothing, really. Some punk just hit me with a wrench and took a few dollars from me. I'm none the worse for wear. The guys down at the cab company have some *real* stories to tell about their experiences. What happened to me—why, it wasn't anything."

I felt ice cold. Somebody had robbed my father! Someone at school had almost scared Mrs. Gottsman to death! What kind of world was this?

I realized that now more than ever I needed to win that scholarship. If I did, then maybe Dad could quit the cab company. The pressure to get money for my college would be off.

Next day at school, I heard that Mrs. Gottsman was still in intensive care. Seeing Dennie's grinning face made the news all the more unbearable. It was as clear as it could be that he had something to do with hurting Mrs. Gottsman. But his parents swore he'd been home all night. They said he'd been grounded since he got in trouble at school. With his parents ready to back him up, Dennie figured he was in the clear.

That day we had a substitute teacher in music. I didn't feel much like singing. I kept thinking about Mrs. Gottsman.

When I met Dina at break, I finally exploded. "I'm furious, Dina. Dennie got away with it!"

"He won't get away with it forever," Dina said.

"Sure he will," I said bitterly. "Don't you

see the way he's smiling? He looks like the cat that ate the canary."

By the time I went to biology class, I was feeling less angry than depressed. For once I let my lab partner do most of the work.

As we were bending over our microscopes, Jan Draper suddenly screamed.

Mr. Samson, our teacher, looked up. "What on earth—"

Jan was acting like someone possessed. She was jumping up and down and shrieking. It was as if she had gone mad!

9 "THERE'S A SPIDER down my blouse!" Jan screamed. She continued to jump up and down and beat at her blouse. Finally she dashed out of the room.

Most of the class started to laugh. That made Mr. Samson, who was already irritated, even angrier. When Jan tried to sneak back into the room, he called to her. "That'll be enough of that nonsense!"

"But, Mr. Samson," Jan said in a shaky voice, "there was a huge spider on me!"

"Well, I hope you squashed it," a girl said.

Jan sheepishly mumbled, "No—I couldn't find it. It must have fallen out."

Mr. Samson shook his head. "Why don't you just try to keep your mind on your work for a change!"

"But, Mr. Samson—"

"That's enough!" Mr. Samson shouted.

Jan went back to her microscope and nervously sat down. From my seat a few feet away, I heard the boy next to her whisper. "I see the spider on your back, Jan," he said.

He was only joking, but Jan took him seriously. She leaped up again with a choked scream. Mr. Samson immediately stood up. "Jan, I want you to leave this classroom at once. And don't come back until you've got yourself under control!"

Jan ran sobbing from the room. Mr. Samson glared at the rest of us. "If I hear one more person laugh, you'll all spend the rest of the period working on a pop quiz!"

Silence fell quickly.

After class, I saw Jan sitting on a bench outside the girls' restroom. I went over and asked how she was.

"It's not fair!" she said angrily. "There *was* a spider on me. It was horrible!"

"Yeah, I guess so," I said.

"You would have screamed, too. Anybody would have," Jan hotly defended herself. "It was so hairy and slimy." She shook at the memory.

Suddenly Jan leaped up. "It's on me

again! I feel it crawling on me!"

"Where, Jan? I don't see it!" I said.

Jan wildly slapped her arms. Then to my astonishment, she tore her blouse right off. She completely ignored the laughter and stares she got from kids passing down the hall. She just continued to slap at her bare arms.

"Help me! Get it off!" she screamed.

But how could I help? *I didn't see a thing.*

And then it came to me. All of a sudden I knew what was wrong with Jan.

I stepped forward and grabbed her arms. Looking straight into her terrified eyes, I said, "You did it, didn't you? You were the one who wrecked Mrs. Gottsman's room and scared her."

Jan's eyes got huge. She was a pretty girl, but now she looked ugly. "You're crazy!" she yelled back.

"You did it," I repeated fiercely.

"You liar!" Jan screeched. Her voice sounded like a fingernail scratching on a chalkboard. It made my skin crawl.

Then down the hallway, I saw Basil. He

was just standing there, staring at Jan.

A funny, unearthly feeling came over me. I knew that something unnatural was happening.

At that moment Mr. Dorman, the vice-principal, came down the hall. "Put your blouse back on!" he ordered.

Jan choked back a sob and hastily put on her blouse again.

"Now, in heaven's name, what's the matter with you?" Mr. Dorman demanded.

Jan started to explain; then she stopped. I could see that she was more embarrassed now than frightened. Finally she said, "It was all just a mistake, Mr. Dorman. I'm sorry. It won't happen again."

With that, she rushed off. As I walked to my next class, I saw she had cornered Dennie at his locker. I heard them fiercely whispering to each other. Without a doubt, Dennie had put Jan up to the cruel joke on Mrs. Gottsman. Now Jan was probably blaming him for the strange things that were happening to her.

After school that day, I saw Basil

heading toward the the parking lot. He waited for me until I caught up. Then we slowly walked across campus.

"Did you hear all that noise Jan was making today?" I asked.

He grimly nodded.

"She was really spooked. She kept claiming there was a spider crawling all over her. But there wasn't. So what do you think made her believe there was?"

"Conscience," he answered simply.

"You mean guilt about Mrs. Gottsman." It wasn't really a question. I knew the answer.

"Yes." He sounded so sure. "Her feelings of guilt turned into something she hates and fears—a spider. And she'll probably continue to feel guilt until she confesses."

I silently stared at Basil. For once there was no warmth in him. His eyes looked hard and cold. They were like brilliant chunks of precious stone.

"Did you cause it to happen, Basil?" I finally asked him.

He shrugged his shoulders. "I told her this morning that whoever had hurt

Mrs. Gottsman had done a wretched thing. I said that Mrs. Gottsman was a good woman who deserved kindness and respect. And I warned Jan that whoever was responsible wouldn't be able to deal with the guilt."

"How did you know it was Jan?"

"A feeling."

Basil had known it was Jan. It could have been Jim Argus or somebody else. But he had *known* it was Jan. And he had caused her to feel so guilty that she imagined that spider.

We halted beside my dreaming tree. I stared at it in the late afternoon sun.

"Just who are you, Basil?" I asked him.

Basil didn't seem to hear me. He placed his palm against the tree and stared up into its dancing branches. "A good solid tree. It's been here a long time. Maybe as long as the school."

I waited for a minute, hoping he still might answer. But when he spoke again, all he said was, "Well, it's getting dark. We'd both better be going home, Valerie."

As I said goodbye, I thought again about

my question. Perhaps I'd asked the wrong thing. Perhaps I should have asked, "Basil, *what* are you?"

I had other questions to think about, too. Was there still any chance I would win that scholarship? Tomorrow the name of the scholarship winner would be announced.

I was extremely nervous when I went to school the next morning. I didn't see how I could wait until the announcement was made at the end of the day.

In biology class I had to try extra hard to concentrate. Mr. Samson was explaining leaf cells. "Why do the leaves change color in the winter?" he asked.

"Because they stop producing food," Jan said. She seemed very calm today. And she was obviously on her best behavior.

"That's right, Jan," Mr. Samson said, a little surprised she had answered.

Suddenly the door opened. Basil entered and carried a message to Mr. Samson's desk. Things like that happened all the time. Students on office duty were always taking messages to teachers or students. Mr. Samson read the message and initialed it.

Basil turned to leave. But as he headed out the door, he stopped for just an instant. He turned and looked right at Jan. Then he left the room.

Jan coughed and looked down at her book. Seeing Basil had clearly upset her.

"In the process of photosynthesis—" Mr. Samson began. But he never finished.

"The mice!" Jan screamed. "They're getting out of their cage!"

Mr. Samson quickly turned and looked at the cage. "It looks perfectly all right to me. Marie, check the cage."

Marie got up and checked. "All the mice are present and accounted for, Mr. Samson."

Everybody laughed at that.

"I saw one of those mice climbing out of the cage!" Jan insisted.

"Maybe it was just a big roach," a tall boy suggested with a laugh. "Lot of roaches around here."

"All right, all right. Settle down!" Mr. Samson yelled. "We've got the entire chapter on photosynthesis to cover. Remember, the test is Wednesday."

I stole another glance at Jan. I saw she was still shaking. Suddenly she let out another cry. "It's on my shoe!" she screamed and jumped up. She knocked over her desk and sent her books flying.

A few kids laughed, but most were scared. They thought Jan was either on drugs or going crazy. It wasn't funny anymore.

"Jan," Mr. Samson said in a calm voice, "I want you to go immediately to the nurse's office."

"The mouse is running up my leg!" Jan screamed.

Mr. Samson was really concerned now. He looked at me. "Valerie, will you take her to the nurse?"

"Sure," I said. I took Jan's arm. "Come on, Jan."

When we were outside the classroom, Jan anxiously turned to me. "The—the mouse. You didn't see it, did you?"

"No, Jan," I said softly.

Jan gripped my shoulder. "He did this to

me! Basil Harris. You'd better stay away from him. He's like that old woman in Salem. The one who made the man choke to death. A devil, that's what he is."

"Oh, Jan, don't be silly."

"It's true! He said something like this would happen. He made it happen."

"Listen, Jan, the only one making it happen is you yourself. It's your own imagination. You're feeling guilty about hurting Mrs. Gottsman. Just admit what you did, Jan. Then you'll feel better."

Jan glanced wildly around. Then she whispered, "But—but they'll kick me out of school. They'll put me in jail. What if she dies? Then what? They'll blame me!"

I had trouble feeling the slightest bit of pity for Jan. She didn't care what happened to poor Mrs. Gottsman. She was just thinking about herself.

"Jan, why did you do such a thing? Mrs. Gottsman never hurt you."

"Dennie asked me. Oh, Val, she kicked him out of music. It wasn't fair. Dennie felt so bad. He asked me to pay her back.

I thought it would be kind of fun to scare her. I didn't think she'd get sick!"

"How come Dennie didn't do his own dirty work?" I asked.

"He couldn't. His parents are watching him like a hawk." Jan reached in her purse and took out a necklace.

"Dennie gave me this. Isn't it pretty? And just for doing him that little favor. It was no big deal. I just put up a few posters. And I put the tape on. I didn't do anything really bad."

We turned the corner and stopped. Basil stood directly in our path.

Jan shrank back. "Stay away! Just stay away from me!" she cried.

Basil stared coldly at her. Then without a word, he passed us by.

"Did you see how he looked at me?" Jan asked me.

"No."

"Those eyes!" Jan began to shake.

"Oh, Jan!"

"Something—something's crawling on my neck!" She grabbed at her neck.

"Jan, come on. We'd better go to

the principal's office. You can tell her everything."

I led her to the office. There I asked the secretary if we could see Ms. Baldwin. As we stepped into Ms. Baldwin's room, I could see Jan was shaking worse than ever.

"Ms. Baldwin, Jan wants to tell you what happened in the music room," I said.

Jan crumpled in a chair. "It's all Dennie's fault," she sobbed. "It wasn't my fault."

As I went back to biology, Jan was telling the whole story.

By early afternoon, both Jan and Dennie were suspended from school. We also heard that Mrs. Gottsman was still in intensive care. She probably wouldn't return to school this semester even if she did get well.

At the end of that very long day, the official announcement came over the PA system. *Hawthorne High was pleased to announce the winner of the scholarship.*

It was Evan Wasserman.

I couldn't cry, but I wanted to. Evan was a fine student, and he deserved it.

But I knew that I would have won if it hadn't been for Ms. Brundage. I'd received the top score on the current affairs test. I'd written a good essay, according to Mrs. Gottsman. And Evan and I had the same grades. I'd lost—and for the wrong reasons.

I hated the thought of going home. I didn't want to break the bad news to my parents. Even after the last sounds of voices on campus had faded, I couldn't make myself leave. I stood by the bike rack and watched the day grow darker.

I remembered that bitter song I had heard the man singing in the coffee shop: *Nobody cares for the quiet man.*

Or woman, I thought.

"Valerie. I'm sorry," Basil said softly. He had been waiting for me in the shadows.

"Sure." I kicked a rock against the bike rack.

"There's so much injustice in the world," he said.

"Yeah," I said.

The silence that fell between us was broken by a car coming around the corner. Basil and I turned at the sound of its screaming brakes. For a panicked moment, I thought of Bob Short. But no, poor Bob was dead.

The car stopped suddenly at the curb. I saw two big guys jump out and come towards us.

I quickly recognized the two. One of them was Dennie. The other looked like his older brother, Keith. I'd seen Keith just a couple times. He was meaner and tougher than Dennie. He'd been in jail twice already.

Both Dennie and Keith were carrying something in their hands. At first I couldn't see what. When I did, I gasped. They had tire chains!

"Basil, get away from here!" I yelled at him.

He didn't move. Maybe it was too late to move. Or maybe Basil didn't want to. He just stood there and watched them come.

10

"WELL," BASIL SAID confidently, "the jackals travel in pairs. And they bring weapons."

Dennie snarled, "We're going to make you wish you were dead, creep! In fact, maybe we can just make your wish come true."

I saw Keith raise the chain. I screamed out a warning. But the blow fell too quickly for Basil to side-step, and his face was slashed. I saw a bloody gash form on his face.

Basil grabbed the chain and yanked it hard. Keith went crashing to the ground and stayed there, stunned. Quickly as I could, I dashed in and grabbed the chain from his hand.

Then Dennie came at Basil. There was murder in his eyes. Basil ducked, and I heard punches. It was a sickening sound.

Finally Dennie landed a blow with the chain. I saw Basil drop to his knees.

At that, I flew at Dennie and tried to tackle him. But since he weighed about seventy pounds more than I did, he had no trouble throwing me off. I hit the ground hard.

But by that time Basil was on his feet again. He threw Dennie into the shrubbery.

Dennie immediately staggered to his feet. He was yelling like a beast. I knew he was going to hurt Basil bad—maybe even kill him.

I turned and stared at Basil. To my horror, I saw that his handsome face was covered with bruises. His nose seemed to be broken.

Then I noticed Keith seemed to be coming around again. I glanced at the chain still in my hand. For one moment, I considered using it.

But I couldn't. Instead, I turned and ran back to the school as fast as I could. I pounded on all the locked doors.

"Somebody help! They're killing him!" I cried.

Two janitors heard me and came

running to the door.

"Two guys are killing somebody out near the parking lot," I screamed.

The janitors grabbed mops as the handiest weapons. Then we all went tearing back to the bike rack. I prayed I wasn't too late.

When we got there, I wasn't prepared for the sight that greeted us. We found Dennie and Keith lying on the grass. They were moaning and their faces were swollen.

"So who is killing who?" one janitor asked me.

"The guy they attacked is gone," I said. I looked for Basil. I expected to see him lying in the shrubbery. But I couldn't find him. His motorcycle was gone, too.

"Well, do you want us to call the cops?" the older janitor asked.

"No—no, I guess not," I said. "It looks like the fight's over."

The janitors helped Dennie and Keith to their feet. The two brothers slowly limped away without a word.

I couldn't believe it! Basil had beaten them both!

But he was hurt, too. I'd seen how badly bruised he was. I had to find out what had happened to him.

As fast as I could, I rode my bike over to Basil's house. All the way there, I kept thinking of how terrible he had looked.

I rang the bell a couple of times before Faith came to the door. "Valerie! What a pleasure to see you again," she said. "Please come in."

"Basil," I gasped breathlessly. "Is he all right?"

"Oh, yes. See for yourself. He's in the garden with his roses."

I hurried around to the back of the house. I found him there, standing in the growing darkness. His back was turned to me as he bent to cut some roses.

"Basil! Basil, are you okay?" I cried.

He turned, and my mouth dropped open in astonishment. There wasn't a mark on his face!

He smiled. "Valerie. I knew you would come. I wanted to talk to you."

"Oh, Basil. Oh, thank God you're okay. But how—I mean, I saw—"

"It was nothing. The wounds were all slight. What matters is you, Valerie."

He reached out and took my hands. "There are few people in this world who really care about others. Those few make up for everyone who doesn't care. You're needed, Valerie. So you mustn't ever lose heart. You can get along without the scholarship. But the world can't get along without you."

I stared into his eyes and blinked back tears. Then he pulled me close and kissed me.

"Valerie, I love you," he said. "And I always will." He picked the largest pink rose and gave it to me.

"Remember me," he said. Then we said goodbye.

I slowly biked home holding the pink rose. I felt unbelievably happy. Just why I felt that way, I couldn't explain. I simply had a feeling I was going to make it.

* * *

I never saw Basil again after that. The next week in school, he wasn't in any of his classes. The school said he had withdrawn suddenly.

At first I thought it strange that he didn't say goodbye to me. Then I realized that he had that moment he gave me the rose.

Still, I couldn't rest without finding out everything I could. So I went to Basil's house.

Faith, as sweet and kind as always, greeted me. When I asked about Basil, she simply said, "He's gone, dear."

"Gone," I softly repeated. "But why so suddenly?"

"Oh, but it wasn't sudden."

"Please, Faith, tell me where he is. What's happened to him?"

"Oh, but Valerie, I think you know the story," Faith said with a smile. "It happened on the twelfth of April in 1891. A terrible fire. He loved his students so much that he died trying to save them. Such a fine, bright man. So young to be a principal."

"No, no, I mean Basil. Not Mr. Hawthorne," I said.

Then Faith took my hand and led me

into her bedroom. She pointed to a large portrait on the wall. There was no doubt in my mind that it was Basil.

"He was just eighteen when he began to teach. And then they made him principal. Have you seen the watch his father gave him?"

I stared at the beautiful watch I'd seen Basil wearing. The initials on the back read "B. H." for Basil Harris. *Or Bill Hawthorne.*

I couldn't keep the tears from filling my eyes. Faith clasped my hand and softly said, "Don't cry. He wouldn't want it. Oh, don't cry. He was someone special. And didn't he leave us something nice? All of us?"

* * *

In the next few days, I was elected student council president to carry on Basil's work. At the council meeting, most kids cheered when I said that Basil had started something good at Hawthorne. And I vowed to continue it.

About a week later, they finally got around to cleaning the statue of

William Evans Hawthorne. Afterwards, the face was still not very clear. But I looked closely and I saw two faces merge into one.

Nevertheless, I never told anybody who Basil really was. I wasn't sure myself, I guess. I only knew that he wasn't an ordinary boy.

If I ever doubted that, I only had to look at my pink rose. That beautiful flower never wilted or lost its lovely scent.

After Basil had first given it to me, I'd taken it to Mrs. Gottsman in the hospital. When she left the hospital two weeks later, she gave the rose back to me. It was still fresh and fragrant.

"I think it is a special rose," she smiled. "And it is meant for you."

Maybe that rose brought me more of Basil's magic. Or maybe I never forgot his advice to me. In any case, I didn't lose heart. And that spring I received a scholarship to a fine midwestern college. There I could specialize in the education of the disabled. Late one night when I felt Basil very close, I went to the bronze statue. I put the rose on the pedestal.

I turned one last time to look at the statue. And the pink rose was gone.